A GARDEN FOR A GROUNDHOG

LORNA BALIAN

ABINGDON PRESS NASHVILLE

A GARDEN FOR A GROUNDHOG

Library of Congress Cataloging in Publication Data

Balian, Lorna.
  A garden for a ground hog.
  Summary: Mr. O'Leary appreciates his groundhog's help in predicting the weather on Groundhog Day but tries to come up with a plan to keep him from eating all the vegetables in his garden.
  1. Children's stories, American.   [1. Woodchuck—Fiction.   2. Groundhog Day—Fiction.   3 Gardens—Fiction]   I. Title.
PZ7.B1978Gar   1985   [E]   84-28233

ISBN 0-687-14009-9

For my friend, Kathy , who knows groundhogs -

and for my grandson, Andre , who doesn't.

The O'Learys had a bit of a farm.
A small cottage for the two of them and their cat,
a tiny shed for the goat, the lamb, and two chickens,
and a tidy little garden – with an apple tree.

It wasn't much of a farm,
but it was enough –
and it belonged to them.

There was also a groundhog.
He didn't belong to anyone – just himself.
He lived in a burrow under the apple tree.

Mrs. O'Leary spent the winter spinning and knitting,
and cooking delicious meals from the food
they had grown in the garden the summer before.
They ate zucchini squash soup with egg dumplings;
zucchini bread with goat cheese and pickled beets;
zucchini casserole with potatoes, peas, and beans;
zucchini salad with yogurt, cabbage, and tomatoes;
and zucchini-carrot cake.

Mr. O'Leary spent the winter reading seed catalogs,
and repairing the garden tools.

The cat spent the winter curled up by the woodstove,
or stretched out on the sunny windowsill.
(That's what cats are supposed to do.)

The goat, the lamb, and the chickens spent the winter
giving milk, growing wool, and laying eggs.
(That's what goats, lambs, and chickens are supposed to do.)

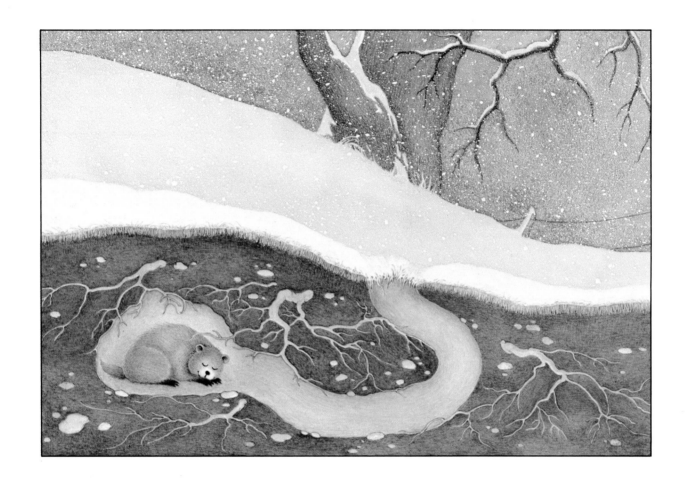

The groundhog spent the winter hibernating in his burrow.
(That's what groundhogs are supposed to do.)

Along about February everyone began feeling restless.
Mrs. O'Leary had used up all of the wool.
Mr. O'Leary had ordered the garden seeds.
The cat dreamed of chasing mice in the fields.

The goat, the lamb, and the chickens
longed to kick up their heels in the grass.

The groundhog was feeling twinges of hunger.
He hadn't eaten anything all winter. (He wasn't supposed to.)

"Tomorrow is Groundhog Day," said Mr. O'Leary. "We must watch for him in the morning. If he comes out and sees his shadow, it will frighten him and he will go back to bed. That will mean six more weeks of winter. If he doesn't see his shadow, he will stay awake. Then spring will be early, and we can plant our garden sooner."

"Such foolishness! When that groundhog comes out of his hole, it's only to see if we have planted anything yet. After all of our work, he ate more from our garden last summer than we did!" said Mrs. O'Leary.

"That's what groundhogs are supposed to do, my dear. They eat all summer so they can sleep all winter. We must allow him some food in exchange for his help in forecasting the weather. I have a plan that will ensure that he eats only what we want him to eat this summer," said Mr. O'Leary.

Groundhog Day found Mr. and Mrs. O'Leary
watching and waiting under the apple tree.

The groundhog stirred himself
and waddled out into the sunshine
to see if the O'Learys' garden was planted yet.
When he realized it wasn't, he tottered back to bed.
(Just as he was supposed to.)

The winter continued and everyone waited.

Eventually – spring arrived.
(Just the way it was supposed to.)

Mr. and Mrs. O'Leary planted their garden.
The cat chased mice.
The goat, the lamb, and the chickens
kicked up their heels in the grass.

The groundhog nibbled alfalfa and dandelions – waiting.

Mr. and Mrs. O'Leary weeded, watered, hoed, and fussed.
(That's what gardeners are supposed to do.)

The garden grew,
(Just as it was supposed to.)
And it was beautiful. There were plump, red tomatoes;
sweet, juicy melons; tender peas and beans; crisp carrots;
big, round cabbages; onions; potatoes; beets; and berries –

all for the O'Learys.

The zucchini squash was for the groundhog.

But groundhogs can't read!
(They're not supposed to.)